Tyndy!

This book takes place in Pee Wee Valley, Kentucky, a little town we O close to the place where your Mother, Uncle Joe and I grew up. I hope you enjoy it.

Merry Christmas (1981).

Love,
Aunt Sarah
&
Uncle Jim

THE
LITTLE COLONEL

Books illustrated by James Rice:

Cajun Night Before Christmas,
by Trosclair

Gaston, the Green-Nosed Alligator,
by James Rice

The Little Colonel,
by Annie Fellows Johnston

Lyn and the Fuzzy, by James Rice

THE
LITTLE COLONEL

BY
ANNIE FELLOWS JOHNSTON

Illustrated by James Rice

PELICAN PUBLISHING COMPANY
GRETNA 1974

Manufactured in the United States of America

Published by Pelican Publishing Company, Inc.
630 Burmaster Street, Gretna, Louisiana 70053

TO

ONE OF KENTUCKY'S

DEAREST LITTLE DAUGHTERS

The Little Colonel

HERSELF — THIS REMEMBRANCE

OF A HAPPY SUMMER IS

AFFECTIONATELY

INSCRIBED

THE
LITTLE COLONEL

CHAPTER I.

IT was one of the prettiest places in all Kentucky where the Little Colonel stood that morning. She was reaching up on tiptoes, her eager little face pressed close against the iron bars of the great entrance gate that led to a fine old estate known as " Locust."

A ragged little Scotch and Skye terrier stood on its hind feet beside her, thrusting his inquisitive nose between the bars, and wagging his tasselled tail in lively approval of the scene before them.

They were looking down a long avenue that stretched for nearly a quarter of a mile between rows of stately old locust-trees.

At the far end they could see the white pillars of a large stone house gleaming through the Virginia creeper that nearly covered it. But they could not see the old Colonel in his big chair on the porch behind the cool screen of vines.

At that very moment he had caught the rattle of wheels along the road, and had picked up his field-glass to see who was passing. It was only a coloured man jogging along in the heat and dust with a cart full of chicken-coops. The Colonel watched him drive up a lane that led to the back of the new hotel that had just been opened in this quiet country place. Then his glance fell on the two small strangers coming through his gate down the avenue toward him. One was the friskiest dog he had ever

seen in his life. The other was a child
he judged to be about five years old.

Her shoes were covered with dust,
and her white sunbonnet had slipped off
and was hanging over her shoulders.
A bunch of wild flowers she had gath-
ered on the way hung limp and faded
in her little warm hand. Her soft, light
hair was cut as short as a boy's.

There was something strangely familiar about the child, especially in the
erect, graceful way she walked.

Old Colonel Lloyd was puzzled. He
had lived all his life in Lloydsborough,
and this was the first time he had ever
failed to recognize one of the neighbours' children. He knew every dog
and horse, too, by sight if not by name.

Living so far from the public road
did not limit his knowledge of what
was going on in the world. A powerful
field-glass brought every passing object

in plain view, while he was saved all annoyance of noise and dust.

"I ought to know that child as well as I know my own name," he said to himself. "But the dog is a stranger in these parts. Liveliest thing I ever set eyes on! They must have come from the hotel. Wonder what they want."

He carefully wiped the lens for a better view. When he looked again he saw that they evidently had not come to visit him.

They had stopped half-way down the avenue, and climbed up on a rustic seat to rest.

The dog sat motionless about two minutes, his red tongue hanging out as if he were completely exhausted.

Suddenly he gave a spring, and bounded away through the tall blue grass. He was back again in a moment, with a stick in his mouth. Standing up with his fore paws in the lap of his little mistress, he looked so wistfully into her face that she could not refuse this invitation for a romp.

The Colonel chuckled as they went tumbling about in the grass to find the stick which the child repeatedly tossed away.

He hitched his chair along to the other end of the porch as they kept getting farther away from the avenue.

It had been many a long year since those old locust-trees had seen a sight like that. Children never played any more under their dignified shadows.

Time had been (but they only whispered this among themselves on rare spring days like this) when the little feet chased each other up and down the long walk, as much at home as the pewees in the beeches.

Suddenly the little maid stood up

straight, and began to sniff the air, as if some delicious odour had blown across the lawn.

" Fritz," she exclaimed, in delight, " I 'mell 'trawberries!"

The Colonel, who could not hear the remark, wondered at the abrupt pause in the game. He understood it, however, when he saw them wading through the tall grass, straight to his strawberry bed. It was the pride of his heart, and the finest for miles around. The first berries of the season had been picked only the day before. Those that now hung temptingly red on the vines he intended to send to his next neighbour, to prove his boasted claim of always raising the finest and earliest fruit.

He did not propose to have his plans spoiled by these stray guests. Laying the field-glass in its accustomed place on the little table beside his chair, he picked up his hat and strode down the walk.

Colonel Lloyd's friends all said he looked like Napoleon, or rather like Napoleon might have looked had he been born and bred a Kentuckian.

He made an imposing figure in his suit of white duck.

The Colonel always wore white from May till October.

There was a military precision about him, from his erect carriage to the cut of the little white goatee on his determined chin.

No one looking into the firm lines of his resolute face could imagine him ever abandoning a purpose or being turned aside when he once formed an opinion.

Most children were afraid of him. The darkies about the place shook in their shoes when he frowned. They had learned from experience that "ole Marse Lloyd had a tigah of a tempah in him."

As he passed down the walk there were two mute witnesses to his old soldier life. A spur gleamed on his boot heel, for he had just returned from his morning ride, and his right sleeve hung empty.

He had won his title bravely. He had given his only son and his strong right arm to the Southern cause. That had been nearly thirty years ago.

He did not charge down on the enemy with his usual force this time. The little head, gleaming like sunshine in the strawberry patch, reminded him so strongly of a little fellow who used to follow him everywhere, — Tom, the sturdiest, handsomest boy in the county,

— Tom, whom he had been so proud of, whom he had so nearly worshipped.

Looking at this fair head bent over the vines, he could almost forget that Tom had ever outgrown his babyhood, that he had shouldered a rifle and followed him to camp, a mere boy, to be shot down by a Yankee bullet in his first battle.

The old Colonel could almost believe he had him back again, and that he stood in the midst of those old days the locusts sometimes whispered about.

He could not hear the happiest of little voices that was just then saying, " Oh, Fritz, isn't you glad we came? An' isn't you glad we've got a gran'fathah with such good 'trawberries? "

It was hard for her to put the " s " before her consonants.

As the Colonel came nearer she tossed another berry into the dog's mouth. A twig snapped, and she raised a startled face toward him.

"Suh?" she said, timidly, for it seemed to her that the stern, piercing eyes had spoken.

"What are you doing here, child?" he asked, in a voice so much kinder than his eyes that she regained her usual self-possession at once.

"Eatin' 'trawberries," she answered, coolly.

"Who are you, anyway?" he exclaimed, much puzzled. As he asked the question his gaze happened to rest on the dog, who was peering at him through the ragged, elfish wisps of hair nearly covering its face, with eyes that were startlingly human.

"'Peak when yo'ah 'poken to, Fritz," she said, severely, at the same time popping another luscious berry into her mouth.

Fritz obediently gave a long yelp. The Colonel smiled grimly.

" What's your name? " he asked, this time looking directly at her.

" Mothah calls me her baby," was the soft-spoken reply, " but papa an' Mom Beck they calls me the Little Cun'l."

" What under the sun do they call you that for? " he roared.

" 'Cause I'm so much like you," was the startling answer.

" Like me! " fairly gasped the Colonel. " How are you like me? "

" Oh, I'm got such a vile tempah, an' I stamps my foot when I gets mad, an' gets all red in the face. An' I hollahs. at folks, an' looks jus' zis way."

She drew her face down and puckered her lips into such a sullen pout that it looked as if a thunder-storm had passed over it. The next instant she smiled up at him serenely.

The Colonel laughed. " What makes you think I am like that?" he said. " You never saw me before."

"Yes, I have too," she persisted. " You's a-hangin' in a gold frame over ou' mantel."

Just then a clear, high voice was heard calling out in the road.

The child started up in alarm. " Oh, deah," she exclaimed in dismay, at sight of the stains on her white dress, where she had been kneeling on the fruit, " that's Mom Beck. Now I'll be tied up, and maybe put to bed for runnin' away again. But the berries is mighty nice," she added, politely. " Good mawnin', suh. Fritz, we mus' be goin' now."

The voice was coming nearer.

" I'll walk down to the gate with you," said the Colonel, anxious to learn something more about his little guest.

"Oh, you'd bettah not, suh!" she cried in alarm. "Mom Beck doesn't like you a bit. She just hates you! She's goin' to give you a piece of her mind the next time she sees you. I heard her tell Aunt Nervy so."

There was as much real distress in the child's voice as if she were telling him of a promised flogging.

"Lloyd! Aw, Lloy-eed!" the call came again.

A neat-looking coloured woman glanced in at the gate as she was passing by, and then stood still in amazement. She had often found her little charge playing along the roadside or hiding behind trees, but she had never before known her to pass through any one's gate.

As the name came floating down to him through the clear air, a change came over the Colonel's stern face. He stooped over the child. His hand trembled as he put it under her soft chin and raised her eyes to his.

"Lloyd, Lloyd!" he repeated, in a puzzled way. "Can it be possible? There certainly is a wonderful resemblance. You have my little Tom's hair, and only my baby Elizabeth ever had such hazel eyes."

He caught her up in his one arm, and strode on to the gate, where the coloured woman stood.

"Why, Becky, is that you?" he cried, recognizing an old, trusted servant who had lived at Locust in his wife's lifetime.

Her only answer was a sullen nod.

"Whose child is this?" he asked, eagerly, without seeming to notice her defiant looks. "Tell me if you can."

"How can I tell you, suh," she demanded, indignantly, "when you have fo'bidden even her name to be spoken befo' you?"

A harsh look came into the Colonel's eyes. He put the child hastily down, and pressed his lips together.

"Don't tie my sunbonnet, Mom Beck," she begged. Then she waved her hand with an engaging smile.

"Good-bye, suh," she said, graciously. "We've had a mighty nice time!"

The Colonel took off his hat with his usual courtly bow, but he spoke no word in reply.

When the last flutter of her dress had disappeared around the bend of the road, he walked slowly back toward the house.

Half-way down the long avenue where she had stopped to rest, he sat down on the same rustic seat. He could feel her soft little fingers resting on his neck, where they had lain when he carried her to the gate.

A very un-Napoleonlike mist blurred his sight for a moment. It had been so long since such a touch had thrilled him, so long since any caress had been given him.

More than a score of years had gone by since Tom had been laid in a soldier's grave, and the years that Elizabeth had been lost to him seemed almost a lifetime.

And this was Elizabeth's little daughter. Something very warm and sweet seemed to surge across his heart as he thought of the Little Colonel. He was glad, for a moment, that they called her that; glad that his only grandchild looked enough like himself for others to see the resemblance.

But the feeling passed as he remembered that his daughter had married against his wishes, and he had closed his doors for ever against her.

The old bitterness came back redoubled in its force.

The next instant he was stamping down the avenue, roaring for Walker, his body-servant, in such a tone that the cook's advice was speedily taken: "Bettah hump yo'self outen dis heah kitchen befo' de ole tigah gits to lashin' roun' any pearter."

CHAPTER II.

MOM BECK carried the ironing - board out of the hot kitchen, set the irons off the stove, and then tiptoed out to the side porch of the little cottage.

"Is yo' head feelin' any bettah, honey?" she said to the pretty, girlish-looking woman lying in the hammock. "I promised to step up to the hotel this evenin' to see one of the chambah-maids. I thought I'd take the Little Cun'l along with me if you was willin'. She's always wild to play with Mrs. Wyford's children up there."

"Yes, I'm better, Becky," was the

languid reply. "Put a clean dress on Lloyd if you are going to take her out."

Mrs. Sherman closed her eyes again, thinking gratefully, "Dear, faithful old Becky! What a comfort she has been all my life, first as my nurse, and now as Lloyd's! She is worth her weight in gold!"

The afternoon shadows were stretching long across the grass when Mom Beck led the child up the green slope in front of the hotel.

The Little Colonel had danced along so gaily with Fritz that her cheeks glowed like wild roses. She made a quaint little picture with such short sunny hair and dark eyes shining out from under the broad-brimmed white hat she wore.

Several ladies who were sitting on the shady piazza, busy with their embroidery, noticed her admiringly.

"It's Elizabeth Lloyd's little daughter," one of them explained. "Don't you remember what a scene there was some years ago when she married a New York man? Sherman, I believe, his name was, Jack Sherman. He was a splendid fellow, and enormously wealthy. Nobody could say a word against him, except that he was a Northerner. That was enough for the old Colonel, though. He hates Yankees like poison. He stormed and swore, and forbade Elizabeth ever coming in his sight again. He had her room locked up, and not a soul on the place ever dares mention her name in his hearing."

The Little Colonel sat down demurely on the piazza steps to wait for the children. The nurse had not finished dressing them for the evening.

She amused herself by showing Fritz

the pictures in an illustrated weekly. It was not long until she began to feel that the ladies were talking about her. She had lived among older people so entirely that her thoughts were much deeper than her baby speeches would lead one to suppose.

She understood dimly, from what she had heard the servants say, that there was some trouble between her mother and grandfather. Now she heard it rehearsed from beginning to end. She could not understand what they meant by "bank failures" and "unfortunate investments," but she understood enough to know that her father had lost nearly all his money, and had gone West to make more.

Mrs. Sherman had moved from their elegant New York home two weeks ago to this little cottage in Lloydsborough that her mother had left her. Instead of the houseful of servants they used to have, there was only faithful Mom Beck to do everything.

There was something magnetic in the child's eyes.

Mrs. Wyford shrugged her shoulders uneasily as she caught their piercing gaze fixed on her.

"I do believe that little witch understood every word I said," she exclaimed.

"Oh, certainly not," was the reassuring answer. "She's such a little thing."

But she had heard it all, and understood enough to make her vaguely unhappy. Going home she did not frisk along with Fritz, but walked soberly by Mom Beck's side, holding tight to the friendly black hand.

"We'll go through the woods," said Mom Beck, lifting her over the fence. "It's not so long that way."

As they followed the narrow, straggling path into the cool dusk of the woods, she began to sing. The crooning chant was as mournful as a funeral dirge.

> "The clouds hang heavy, an' it's gwine to rain.
>   Fa'well, my dyin' friends.
> I'm gwine to lie in the silent tomb.
>   Fa'well, my dyin' friends."

A muffled little sob made her stop and look down in surprise.

"Why, what's the mattah, honey?" she exclaimed. "Did Emma Louise make you mad? Or is you cryin' 'cause you're so ti'ed? Come! Ole Becky'll tote her baby the rest of the way."

She picked the light form up in her arms, and, pressing the troubled little face against her shoulder, resumed her walk and her song.

> "It's a world of trouble we're travellin' through.
>   Fa'well, my dyin' friends."

"Oh, don't, Mom Beck," sobbed the child, throwing her arms around the woman's neck, and crying as though her heart would break.

"Land sakes, what is the mattah?" she asked, in alarm. She sat down on a mossy log, took off the white hat, and looked into the flushed, tearful face.

"Oh, it makes me so lonesome when you sing that way," wailed the Little Colonel. "I just can't 'tand it! Mom Beck, is my mothah's heart all broken? Is that why she is sick so much, and will it kill her suah 'nuff?"

"Who's been tellin' you such nonsense?" asked the woman, sharply.

"Some ladies at the hotel were talkin' about it. They said that gran'fathah didn't love her any moah, an' it was just a-killin' her." Mom Beck frowned fiercely.

The child's grief was so deep and intense that she did not know just how to quiet her. Then she said, decidedly, "Well, if that's all that's a-troublin' you, you can jus' get down an' walk home on yo' own laigs. Yo' mamma's a-grievin' 'cause yo' papa has to be away all the time. She's all wo'n out, too, with the work of movin', when she's nevah been used to doin' anything. But her heart isn't broke any moah'n my neck is."

The positive words and the decided toss Mom Beck gave her head settled the matter for the Little Colonel. She wiped her eyes and stood up much relieved.

"Don't you nevah go to worryin' 'bout what you heahs," continued the woman. "I tell you p'intedly you cyarnt nevah b'lieve what you heahs."

"Why doesn't gran'fathah love my mothah?" asked the child, as they came in sight of the cottage. She had puzzled over the knotty problem all the way home. "How can papas not love their little girls?"

" 'Cause he's stubbo'n," was the unsatisfactory answer. "All the Lloyds is. Yo' mamma's stubbo'n, an' you's stubbo'n — "

"I'm not!" shrieked the Little Colonel, stamping her foot. "You sha'n't call me names!"

Then she saw a familiar white hand waving to her from the hammock, and she broke away from Mom Beck with very red cheeks and very bright eyes.

Cuddled close in her mother's arms, she had a queer feeling that she had grown a great deal older in that short afternoon.

Maybe she had. For the first time in her little life she kept her troubles to herself, and did not once mention the thought that was uppermost in her mind.

" Yo' great-aunt Sally Tylah is comin' this mawnin'," said Mom Beck, the day after their visit to the hotel. " Do fo' goodness' sake keep yo'self clean. I'se got too many spring chickens to dress to think 'bout dressin' you up again."

" Did I evah see her befo'? " questioned the Little Colonel.

" Why, yes, the day we moved heah. Don't you know she came and stayed so long, and the rockah broke off the little white rockin'-chair when she sat down in it? "

" Oh, now I know! " laughed the child. " She's the big fat one with curls hangin' round her yeahs like shavin's. I don't like her, Mom Beck. She keeps a-kissin' me all the time, an' a-'queezin' me, an' tellin' me to sit on her lap an' be a little lady. Mom Beck, I de'pise to be a little lady."

There was no answer to her last remark. Mom Beck had stepped into the pantry for more eggs for the cake she was making.

"Fritz," said the Little Colonel, "yo' great-aunt Sally Tylah's comin' this mawnin', an' if you don't want to say 'howdy' to her you'll have to come with me."

A few minutes later a resolute little figure squeezed between the palings of the garden fence down by the gooseberry bushes.

"Now walk on your tiptoes, Fritz!" commanded the Little Colonel, "else somebody will call us back."

Mom Beck, busy with her extra baking, supposed she was with her mother on the shady, vine-covered porch.

She would not have been singing

quite so gaily if she could have seen half a mile up the road.

The Little Colonel was sitting in the weeds by the railroad track, deliberately taking off her shoes and stockings.

"Just like a little niggah," she said, delightedly, as she stretched out her bare feet. "Mom Beck says I ought to know bettah. But it does feel so good!"

No telling how long she might have sat there enjoying the forbidden pleasure of dragging her rosy toes through the warm dust, if she had not heard a horse's hoof-beats coming rapidly along.

"Fritz, it's gran'fathah," she whispered, in alarm, recognizing the erect figure of the rider in its spotless suit of white duck.

"Sh! lie down in the weeds, quick! Lie down, I say!"

They both made themselves as flat as possible, and lay there panting with the exertion of keeping still.

Presently the Little Colonel raised her head cautiously.

"Oh, he's gone down that lane!" she exclaimed. "Now you can get up." After a moment's deliberation she asked, "Fritz, would you rathah have some 'trawberries an' be tied up fo' runnin' away, or not be tied up and not have any of those nice tas'en 'trawberries?"

CHAPTER III.

WO hours later, Colonel Lloyd, riding down the avenue under the locusts, was surprised by a novel sight on his stately front steps.

Three little darkies and a big flop-eared hound were crouched on the bottom step, looking up at the Little Colonel, who sat just above them.

She was industriously stirring something in an old rusty pan with a big, battered spoon.

"Now, May Lilly," she ordered, speaking to the largest and blackest of the group, "you run an' find some nice 'mooth pebbles to put in for raisins.

Henry Clay, you go get me some moah sand. This is 'most too wet."

"Here, you little pickaninnies!" roared the Colonel, as he recognized the cook's children. "What did I tell you about playing around here, tracking dirt all over my premises? You just chase back to the cabin where you belong!"

The sudden call startled Lloyd so that she dropped the pan, and the great mud pie turned upside down on the white steps.

"Well, you're a pretty sight!" said the Colonel, as he glanced with disgust from her soiled dress and muddy hands to her bare feet.

He had been in a bad humour all morning. The sight of the steps covered with sand and muddy tracks gave him an excuse to give vent to his cross feelings.

It was one of his theories that a little

girl should always be kept as fresh and dainty as a flower. He had never seen his own little daughter in such a plight as this, and she had never been allowed to step outside of her own room without her shoes and stockings.

"What does your mother mean," he cried, savagely, "by letting you run barefooted around the country just like poor white trash? An' what are you playing with low-flung niggers for? Haven't you ever been taught any better? I suppose it's some of your father's miserable Yankee notions."

May Lilly, peeping around the corner of the house, rolled her frightened eyes from one angry face to the other. The same temper that glared from the face of the man, sitting erect in his saddle, seemed to be burning in the eyes of the child, who stood, so defiantly before him.

The same kind of scowl drew their eyebrows together darkly.

" Don't you talk that way to me," cried the Little Colonel, trembling with a wrath she did not know how to express.

Suddenly she stooped, and snatching both hands full of mud from the overturned pie, flung it wildly over the spotless white coat.

Colonel Lloyd gasped with astonishment. It was the first time in his life he had ever been openly defied. The next moment his anger gave way to amusement.

" By George! " he chuckled, admiringly. " The little thing has got spirit, sure enough. She's a Lloyd through and through. So that's why they call her ' Little Colonel,' is it? "

There was a tinge of pride in the look he gave her haughty little head and flashing eyes.

"There, there, child!" he said, soothingly. "I didn't mean to make you mad, when you were good enough to come and see me. It isn't often I have a little lady like you pay me a visit."

"I didn't come to see you, suh," she answered, indignantly, as she started toward the gate. "I came to see May Lilly. But I nevah would have come inside yo' gate if I'd known you was goin' to hollah at me an' be so cross."

She was walking off with the air of an offended queen, when the Colonel remembered that if he allowed her to go away in that mood she would probably never set foot on his grounds again. Her display of temper had interested him immensely.

Now that he had laughed off his ill humour, he was anxious to see what other traits of character she possessed.

He wheeled his horse across the walk to bar her way, and quickly dismounted.

"Oh, now, wait a minute," he said, in a coaxing tone. "Don't you want a nice big saucer of strawberries and cream before you go? Walker's picking some now. And you haven't seen my hot-house. It's just full of the loveliest flowers you ever saw. You like roses, don't you, and pinks and lilies and pansies?"

He saw he had struck the right chord as soon as he mentioned the flowers. The sullen look vanished as if by magic. Her face changed as suddenly as an April day.

"Oh, yes!" she cried, with a beaming smile. "I loves 'm bettah than anything!"

He tied his horse, and led the way to the conservatory. He opened the door for her to pass through, and then watched her closely to see what impression it would make on her. He had expected a delighted exclamation of surprise, for he had good reason to be proud of his rare plants. They were arranged with a true artist's eye for colour and effect.

She did not say a word for a moment, but drew a long breath, while the delicate pink in her cheeks deepened and her eyes lighted up. Then she began going slowly from flower to flower, laying her face against the cool, velvety purple of the pansies, touching the roses with her lips, and tilting the white lily-cups to look into their golden depths.

As she passed from one to another as lightly as a butterfly might have done, she began chanting in a happy undertone.

Ever since she had learned to talk she had a quaint little way of singing to herself. All the names that pleased her fancy she strung together in a crooning melody of her own.

There was no special tune. It sounded happy, although nearly always in a minor key.

" Oh, the jonquils an' the lilies! " she sang. " All white an' gold an' yellow. Oh, they're all a-smilin' at me, an' a-sayin' howdy! howdy! "

She was so absorbed in her intense enjoyment that she forgot all about the old Colonel. She was wholly unconscious that he was watching or listening.

" She really does love them," he thought, complacently. " To see her face one would think she had found a fortune."

It was another bond between them.

After awhile he took a small basket from the wall, and began to fill it with his choicest blooms.

"You shall have these to take home," he said. "Now come into the house and get your strawberries."

She followed him reluctantly, turning back several times for one more long sniff of the delicious fragrance.

She was not at all like the Colonel's ideal of what a little girl should be, as she sat in one of the high, stiff chairs, enjoying her strawberries. Her dusty little toes wriggled around in the curls on Fritz's back, as she used him for a footstool. Her dress was draggled and dirty, and she kept leaning over to give the dog berries and cream from the spoon she was eating with herself.

He forgot all this, however, when she began to talk to him.

"My great-aunt Sally Tylah is to ou' house this mawnin'," she announced, confidentially. "That's why we came off. Do you know my Aunt Sally Tylah?"

"Well, slightly!" chuckled the Colonel. "She was my wife's half - sister. So you don't like her, eh? Well, I don't like her either."

He threw back his head and laughed heartily. The more the child talked the more entertaining he found her. He did not remember when he had ever been so amused before as he was by this tiny counterpart of himself.

When the last berry had vanished, she slipped down from the tall chair.

"Do you 'pose it's very late?" she asked, in an anxious voice. "Mom Beck will be comin' for me soon."

"Yes, it is nearly noon," he answered. "It didn't do much good to run away from your Aunt Tyler; she'll see you after all."

"Well, she can't 'queeze me an' kiss

me, 'cause I've been naughty, an' I'll be put to bed like I was the othah day, just as soon as I get home. I 'most wish I was there now," she sighed. "It's so fa' an' the sun's so hot. I lost my sunbonnet when I was comin' heah, too."

Something in the tired, dirty face prompted the old Colonel to say, "Well, my horse hasn't been put away yet. I'll take you home on Maggie Boy."

The next moment he repented making such an offer, thinking what the neighbours might say if they should meet him on the road with Elizabeth's child in his arm.

But it was too late. He could not unclasp the trusting little hand that was slipped in his. He could not cloud the happiness of the eager little face by retracting his promise.

He swung himself into the saddle, with her in front.

Then he put his one arm around her with a firm clasp, as he reached forward to take the bridle.

"You couldn't take Fritz on behin', could you?" she asked, anxiously. "He's mighty ti'ed too."

"No," said the Colonel, with a laugh. "Maggie Boy might object and throw us all off."

Hugging her basket of flowers close in her arms, she leaned her head against him contentedly as they cantered down the avenue.

"Look!" whispered all the locusts, waving their hands to each other excitedly. "Look! The master has his own again. The dear old times are coming back to us."

"How the trees blow!" exclaimed the child, looking up at the green arch overhead. "See! They's all a-noddin' to each othah."

"We'll have to get my shoes an' 'tockin's," she said, presently, when they were nearly home. "They're in that fence cawnah behin' a log."

The Colonel obediently got down and handed them to her. As he mounted again he saw a carriage coming toward them. He recognized one of his nearest neighbours. Striking the astonished Maggie Boy with his spur, he turned her across the railroad track, down the steep embankment, and into an unfrequented lane.

"This road is just back of your garden," he said. "Can you get through the fence if I take you there?"

"That's the way we came out," was the answer. "See that hole where the palin's are off?"

Just as he was about to lift her down, she put one arm around his neck, and kissed him softly on the cheek.

" Good-bye, gran'fatha'," she said, in her most winning way. "I've had a mighty nice time." Then she added, in a lower tone, " 'Kuse me fo' throwin' mud on yo' coat."

He held her close a moment, thinking nothing had ever before been half so sweet as the way she called him grandfather.

From that moment his heart went out to her as it had to little Tom and Elizabeth. It made no difference if her mother had forfeited his love. It made no difference if Jack Sherman was her father, and that the two men heartily hated each other.

It was his own little grandchild he held in his arms.

She had sealed the relationship with a trusting kiss.

" Child," he said, huskily, " you will come and see me again, won't you, no matter if they do tell you not to? You shall have all the flowers and berries you want, and you can ride Maggie Boy as often as you please."

She looked up into his face. It was very familiar to her. She had looked at his portrait often, unconsciously recognizing a kindred spirit that she longed to know.

Her ideas of grandfathers, gained from stories and observation, led her to class them with fairy godmothers. She had always wished for one.

The day they moved to Lloydsborough, Locust had been pointed out to her as her grandfather's home. From that time on she slipped away with Fritz on every possible occasion to peer through the gate, hoping for a glimpse of him.

" Yes, I'll come suah! " she promised. " I likes you just lots, gran'fathah! "

He watched her scramble through the hole in the fence. Then he turned his horse's head slowly homeward.

A scrap of white lying on the grass attracted his attention as he neared the gate.

"It's the lost sunbonnet," he said, with a smile. He carried it into the house, and hung it on the hat-rack in the wide front hall.

"Ole marse is crosser'n two sticks," growled Walker to the cook at dinner. "There ain't no livin' with him. What do you s'pose is the mattah?"

CHAPTER IV.

OM BECK was busy putting lunch on the table when the Little Colonel looked in at the kitchen door.

So she did not see a little tramp, carrying her shoes in one hand, and a basket in the other, who paused there a moment. But when she took up the pan of beaten biscuit she was puzzled to find that several were missing.

"It beats my time," she said, aloud. "The parrot couldn't have reached them, an' Lloyd an' the dog have been in the pa'lah all mawnin'. Somethin' has jus' natch'ly done sperrited 'em away."

Fritz was gravely licking his lips, and the Little Colonel had her mouth full, when they suddenly made their appearance on the front porch.

Aunt Sally Tyler gave a little shriek, and stopped rocking.

"Why, Lloyd Sherman!" gasped her mother, in dismay. "Where have you been? I thought you were with Becky all the time. I was sure I heard you singing out there a little while ago."

"I've been to see my gran'fathah," said the child, speaking very fast. "I made mud pies on his front 'teps, an' we both of us got mad, an' I throwed mud on him, an' he gave me some 'traw-berries an' all these flowers, an' brought me home on Maggie Boy."

She stopped out of breath.

Mrs. Tyler and her niece exchanged astonished glances.

"But, baby, how could you disgrace mother so by going up there looking like a dirty little beggar?"

"He didn't care," replied Lloyd, calmly. "He made me promise to come again, no mattah if you all did tell me not to."

Just then Becky announced that lunch was ready, and carried the child away to make her presentable.

To Lloyd's great surprise she was not put to bed, but was allowed to go to the table as soon as she was dressed. It was not long until she had told every detail of the morning's experience.

While she was taking her afternoon nap, the two ladies sat out on the porch, gravely discussing all she had told them.

"It doesn't seem right for me to allow her to go there," said Mrs. Sherman, "after the way papa has treated us. I can never forgive him for all the terrible things he has said about Jack, and I know Jack can never be friends with him on account of what he has said about me. He has been so harsh and unjust that I don't want my little Lloyd to have anything to do with him. I wouldn't for worlds have him think that I encouraged her going there."

"Well, yes, I know," answered her aunt, slowly. "But there are some things to consider besides your pride, Elizabeth. There's the child herself, you know. Now that Jack has lost so much, and your prospects are so uncertain, you ought to think of her interests. It would be a pity for Locust to go to strangers when it has been in your family for so many generations. That's what it certainly will do unless something turns up to interfere. Old Judge

Woodard told me himself that your father had made a will, leaving everything he owns to some medical institution. Imagine Locust being turned into a sanitarium or a training - school for nurses!"

"Dear old place!" said Mrs. Sherman, with tears in her eyes. "No one ever had a happier childhood than I passed under these old locusts. Every tree seems like a friend. I would be glad for Lloyd to enjoy the place as I did."

"I'd let her go as much as she pleases, Elizabeth. She's so much like the old Colonel that they ought to understand each other, and get along capitally. Who knows, it might end in you all making up some day."

Mrs. Sherman raised her head haughtily. "No, indeed, Aunt Sally. I can forgive and forget much, but you are greatly mistaken if you think I can go to such lengths as that. He closed his doors against me with a curse, for no reason on earth but that the man I loved was born north of the Mason and Dixon line. There never was a nobler man living than Jack, and papa would have seen it if he hadn't deliberately shut his eyes and refused to look at him. He was just prejudiced and stubborn."

Aunt Sally said nothing, but her thoughts took the shape of Mom Beck's declaration, "The Lloyds is all stubbo'n."

"I wouldn't go through his gate now if he got down on his knees and begged me," continued Elizabeth, hotly.

"It's too bad," exclaimed her aunt; "he was always so perfectly devoted to 'little daughter,' as he used to call you. I don't like him myself. We never could get along together at all, because he is so high-strung and overbearing. But I know it would have made your poor mother mighty unhappy if she could have foreseen all this."

Elizabeth sat with the tears dropping down on her little white hands, as her aunt proceeded to work on her sympathies in every way she could think of.

Presently Lloyd came out all fresh and rosy from her long nap, and went to play in the shade of the great beech-trees that guarded the cottage.

"I never saw a child with such influence over animals," said her mother, as Lloyd came around the house with the parrot perched on the broom she was carrying. "She'll walk right up to any strange dog and make friends with it, no matter how savage-looking it is. And there's Polly, so old and cross that she screams and scolds dreadfully if any of us go near her. But Lloyd dresses her up in doll's clothes, puts paper bonnets on her, and makes her just as uncomfortable as she pleases. Look! that is one of her favourite amusements."

The Little Colonel squeezed the parrot into a tiny doll carriage, and began to trundle it back and forth as fast as she could run.

"Ha! ha!" screamed the bird. "Polly is a lady! Oh, Lordy! I'm so happy!"

"She caught that from the washerwoman," laughed Mrs. Sherman. "I should think the poor thing would be dizzy from whirling around so fast."

"Quit that, chillun; stop yo' fussin'," screamed Polly, as Lloyd grabbed her up and began to pin a shawl around her neck. She clucked angrily, but never once attempted to snap at the dimpled fingers that squeezed her tight.

Suddenly, as if her patience was completely exhausted, she uttered a disdainful " Oh, pshaw! " and flew up into an old cedar-tree.

" Mothah! Polly won't play with me any moah," shrieked the child, flying into a rage. She stamped and scowled and grew red in the face. Then she began beating the trunk of the tree with the old broom she had been carrying.

" Did you ever see anything so much like the old Colonel? " said Mrs. Tyler, in astonishment. " I wonder if she acted that way this morning."

" I don't doubt it at all," answered Mrs. Sherman. " She'll be over it in just a moment. These little spells never last long."

Mrs. Sherman was right. In a few moments Lloyd came up the walk, singing.

" I wish you'd tell me a pink story,"

she said, coaxingly, as she leaned against her mother's knee.

"Not now, dear; don't you see that I am busy talking to Aunt Sally? Run and ask Mom Beck for one."

"What on earth does she mean by a pink story?" asked Mrs. Tyler.

"Oh, she is so fond of colours. She is always asking for a pink or a blue or a white story. She wants everything in the story tinged with whatever colour she chooses,—dresses, parasols, flowers, sky, even the icing on the cakes and the paper on the walls."

"What an odd little thing she is!" exclaimed Mrs. Tyler. "Isn't she lots of company for you?"

She need not have asked that question if she could have seen them that evening, sitting together in the early twilight.

Lloyd was in her mother's lap, leaning her head against her shoulder as they rocked slowly back and forth on the dark porch.

There was an occasional rattle of wheels along the road, a twitter of sleepy birds, a distant croaking of frogs.

Mom Beck's voice floated in from the kitchen, where she was stepping briskly around.

" Oh, the clouds hang heavy, an' it's gwine to rain.
   Fa'well, my dyin' friends."

she sang.

Lloyd put her arms closer around her mother's neck.

" Let's talk about Papa Jack," she said. " What you 'pose he's doin' now, 'way out West? "

Elizabeth, feeling like a tired, home-sick child herself, held her close, and was comforted as she listened to the sweet little voice talking about the absent father.

The moon came up after awhile, and streamed in through the vines of the porch. The hazel eyes slowly closed as Elizabeth began to hum an old-time negro lullaby.

"Wondah if she'll run away to-morrow," whispered Mom Beck, as she came out to carry her in the house.

"Who'd evah think now, lookin' at her pretty, innocent face, that she could be so naughty? Bless her little soul!"

The kind old black face was laid lovingly a moment against the fair, soft cheek of the Little Colonel. Then she lifted her in her strong arms, and carried her gently away to bed.

CHAPTER V.

SUMMER lingers long among the Kentucky hills. Each passing day seemed fairer than the last to the Little Colonel, who had never before known anything of country life.

Roses climbed up and almost hid the small white cottage. Red birds sang in the woodbine. Squirrels chattered in the beeches. She was out-of-doors all day long.

Sometimes she spent hours watching the ants carry away the sugar she sprinkled for them. Sometimes she caught flies for an old spider that had his den under the porch steps.

" He is an ogah " (ogre), she explained to Fritz. " He's bewitched me so's I have to kill whole families of flies for him to eat."

She was always busy and always happy.

Before June was half over it got to be a common occurrence for Walker to ride up to the gate on the Colonel's horse. The excuse was always to have a passing word with Mom Beck. But before he rode away, the Little Colonel was generally mounted in front of him. It was not long before she felt almost as much at home at Locust as she did at the cottage.

The neighbours began to comment on it after awhile. " He will surely make up with Elizabeth at this rate," they said. But at the end of the summer the father and daughter had not even had a passing glimpse of each other.

One day, late in September, as the Little Colonel clattered up and down the hall with her grandfather's spur buckled on her tiny foot, she called back over her shoulder: "Papa Jack's comin' home to-morrow."

The Colonel paid no attention.

"I say," she repeated, "Papa Jack's comin' home to-morrow."

"Well," was the gruff response. "Why couldn't he stay where he was? I suppose you won't want to come here any more after he gets back."

"No, I 'pose not," she answered, so carelessly that he was conscious of a very jealous feeling.

"Chilluns always like to stay with their fathahs when they's nice as my Papa Jack is."

The old man growled something behind his newspaper that she did not hear. He would have been glad to choke this man who had come between him and his only child, and he hated him worse than ever when he realized what a large place he held in Lloyd's little heart.

She did not go back to Locust the next day, nor for weeks after that.

She was up almost as soon as Mom Beck next morning, thoroughly enjoying the bustle of preparation.

She had a finger in everything, from polishing the silver to turning the ice-cream freezer.

Even Fritz was scrubbed till he came out of his bath with his curls all white and shining. He was proud of himself, from his silky bangs to the tip of his tasselled tail.

Just before train time, the Little Colonel stuck his collar full of late pink roses, and stood back to admire the effect. Her mother came to the door, dressed for the evening. She wore an airy-looking dress of the palest, softest blue. There was a white rosebud caught in her dark hair. A bright colour, as fresh as Lloyd's own, tinged her cheeks, and the glad light in her brown eyes made them unusually brilliant.

Lloyd jumped up and threw her arms about her. "Oh, mothah," she cried, "you an' Fritz is so bu'ful!"

The engine whistled up the road at the crossing. "Come, we have just time to get to the station," said Mrs. Sherman, holding out her hand.

They went through the gate, down the narrow path that ran beside the dusty road. The train had just stopped in front of the little station when they reached it.

A number of gentlemen, coming out from the city to spend Sunday at the hotel, came down the steps.

They glanced admiringly from the beautiful, girlish face of the mother to the happy child dancing impatiently up and down at her side. They could not help smiling at Fritz as he frisked about in his imposing rose-collar.

"Why, where's Papa Jack?" asked Lloyd, in distress, as passenger after passenger stepped down. "Isn't he goin' to come?"

The tears were beginning to gather in her eyes, when she saw him in the door of the car; not hurrying along to meet them as he always used to come, so full of life and vigour, but leaning heavily on the porter's shoulder, looking very pale and weak.

Lloyd looked up at her mother, from whose face every particle of colour had faded. Mrs. Sherman gave a low, frightened cry as she sprang forward to meet him.

"Oh, Jack! what is the matter? What has happened to you?" she exclaimed, as he took her in his arms. The train had gone on, and they were left alone on the platform.

"Just a little sick spell," he answered, with a smile. "We had a fire out at the mines, and I overtaxed myself some. I've had fever ever since, and it has pulled me down considerably."

"I must send somebody for a carriage," she said, looking around anxiously.

"No, indeed," he protested. "It's only a few steps; I can walk it as well as not. The sight of you and the baby has made me stronger already."

He sent a coloured boy on ahead with his valise, and they walked slowly up the path, with Fritz running wildly around them, barking a glad welcome.

"How sweet and homelike it all

looks!'" he said, as he stepped into the hall, where Mom Beck was just lighting the lamps. Then he sank down on the couch, completely exhausted, and wearily closed his eyes.

The Little Colonel looked at his white face in alarm. All the gladness seemed to have been taken out of the homecoming.

Her mother was busy trying to make him comfortable, and paid no attention to the disconsolate little figure wandering about the house alone. Mom Beck had gone for the doctor.

The supper was drying up in the warming - oven. The ice - cream was melting in the freezer. Nobody seemed to care. There was no one to notice the pretty table with its array of flowers and cut glass and silver.

When Mom Beck came back, Lloyd ate all by herself, and then sat out on the kitchen door-step while the doctor made his visit.

She was just going mournfully off to bed with an aching lump in her throat, when her mother opened the door.

"Come tell papa good-night," she said. "He's lots better now."

She climbed up on the bed beside him, and buried her face on his shoulder to hide the tears she had been trying to keep back all evening.

"How the child has grown!" he exclaimed. "Do you notice, Beth, how much plainer she talks? She does not seem at all like the baby I left last spring. Well, she'll soon be six years old, — a real little woman. She'll be papa's little comfort."

The ache in her throat was all gone after that. She romped with Fritz all the time she was undressing.

Papa Jack was worse next morning.

It was hard for Lloyd to keep quiet when the late September sunshine was so gloriously yellow and the whole outdoors seemed so wide awake.

She tiptoed out of the darkened room where her father lay, and swung on the front gate until she saw the doctor riding up on his bay horse. It seemed to her that the day never would pass.

Mom Beck, rustling around in her best dress ready for church, that afternoon, took pity on the lonesome child.

" Go get yo' best hat, honey," she said, " an' I'll take you with me."

It was one of the Little Colonel's greatest pleasures to be allowed to go to the coloured church.

She loved to listen to the singing, and would sit perfectly motionless while the sweet voices blended like the chords of some mighty organ as they sent the old hymns rolling heavenward.

Service had already commenced by the time they took their seats. Nearly everybody in the congregation was swaying back and forth in time to the mournful melody of " Sinnah, sinnah, where's you boun'? "

One old woman across the aisle began clapping her hands together, and repeated in a singsong tone, " Oh, Lordy! I'm so happy! "

" Why, that's just what our parrot says," exclaimed Lloyd, so much surprised that she spoke right out loud.

Mom Beck put her handkerchief over her mouth, and a general smile went around.

After that the child was very quiet until the time came to take the collection. She always enjoyed this part of the service more than anything else. Instead of passing baskets around, each person was invited to come forward and lay his offering on the table.

Woolly heads wagged, and many feet kept time to the tune:

> "Oh! I'se boun' to git to glory.
>   Hallelujah! Le' me go!"

The Little Colonel proudly marched up with Mom Beck's contribution, and then watched the others pass down the aisle. One young girl in a gorgeously trimmed dress paraded up to the table several times, singing at the top of her voice.

"Look at that good-fo'-nothin' Lize Richa'ds," whispered Mom Beck's nearest neighbour, with a sniff. "She done got a nickel changed into pennies so she could ma'ch up an' show herself five times."

It was nearly sundown when they started home. A tall coloured man, wearing a high silk hat and carrying a gold-headed cane, joined them on the way out.

"Howdy, Sistah Po'tah," he said, gravely shaking hands. "That was a fine disco'se we had the pleasuah of listenin' to this evenin'."

"'Deed it was, Brothah Fostah," she answered. "How's all up yo' way?"

The Little Colonel, running on after a couple of white butterflies, paid no attention to the conversation until she heard her own name mentioned.

"Mistah Sherman came home last night, I heah."

"Yes, but not to stay long, I'm afraid. He's a mighty sick man, if I'm any judge. He's down with fevah, — regulah typhoid. He doesn't look to me like he's long for this world. What's to become of poah Miss 'Lizabeth if that's the case, is moah'n I know."

"We mustn't cross the bridge till we come to it, Sistah Po'tah," he suggested.

"I know that; but a lookin'-glass broke yeste'day mawnin' when nobody had put fingah on it. An' his picture fell down off the wall while I was sweepin' the pa'lah. Pete said his dawg done howl all night last night, an' I've dremp three times hand runnin' 'bout muddy watah."

Mom Beck felt a little hand clutch her skirts, and turned to see a frightened little face looking anxiously up at her.

"Now, what's the mattah with you, honey?" she asked. "I'm only a-tellin' Mistah Fostah about some silly old signs my mammy used to believe in. But they don't mean nothin' at all."

Lloyd couldn't have told why she was

unhappy. She had not understood all that Mom Beck had said, but her sensitive little mind was shadowed by a foreboding of trouble.

The shadow deepened as the days passed. Papa Jack got worse instead of better. There were times when he did not recognize any one, and talked wildly of things that had happened out at the mines.

All the long, beautiful October went by, and still he lay in the darkened room. Lloyd wandered listlessly from place to place, trying to keep out of the way, and to make as little trouble as possible.

"I'm a real little woman now," she repeated, proudly, whenever she was allowed to pound ice or carry fresh water. "I'm papa's little comfort."

One cold, frosty evening she was standing in the hall, when the doctor came out of the room and began to put on his overcoat.

Her mother followed him to take his directions for the night.

He was an old friend of the family's. Elizabeth had climbed on his knees many a time when she was a child. She loved this faithful, white-haired old doctor almost as dearly as she had her father.

"My daughter," he said, kindly, laying his hand on her shoulder, "you are wearing yourself out, and will be down yourself if you are not careful. You must have a professional nurse. No telling how long this is going to last. As soon as Jack is able to travel you must have a change of climate."

Her lips trembled. "We can't afford it, doctor," she said. "Jack has been too sick from the very first to talk about business. He always said a woman should not be worried with such matters, anyway. I don't know what arrangements he has made out West. For all I know, the little I have in my purse now may be all that stands between us and the poorhouse."

The doctor drew on his gloves.

" Why don't you tell your father how matters are? " he asked.

Then he saw he had ventured a step too far.

" I believe Jack would rather die than take help from his hands," she answered, drawing herself up proudly. Her eyes flashed. " I would, too, as far as I am concerned myself."

Then a tender look came over her pale, tired face, as she added, gently, " But I'd do anything on earth to help Jack get well."

The doctor cleared his throat vigorously, and bolted out with a gruff good night. As he rode past Locust, he took solid satisfaction in shaking his fist at the light in an upper window.

CHAPTER VI.

THE Little Colonel followed her mother to the dining-room, but paused on the threshold as she saw her throw herself into Mom Beck's arms and burst out crying.

"Oh, Becky!" she sobbed, "what is going to become of us? The doctor says we must have a professional nurse, and we must go away from here soon. There are only a few dollars left in my purse, and I don't know what we'll do when they are gone. I just know Jack is going to die, and then I'll die, too, and then what will become of the baby?"

Mom Beck sat down, and took the trembling form in her arms.

"There, there!" she said, soothingly, "have yo' cry out. It will do you good. Poah chile! all wo'n out with watchin' an' worry. Ne'm min', ole Becky is as good as a dozen nuhses yet. I'll get Judy to come up an' look aftah the kitchen. An' nobody ain' gwine to die, honey. Don't you go to slayin' all you's got befo' you's called on to do it. The good Lawd is goin' to pahvide fo' us same as Abraham."

The last Sabbath's sermon was still fresh in her mind.

"If we only hold out faithful, there's boun' to be a ram caught by the hawns some place, even if we haven't got eyes to see through the thickets. The Lawd will pahvide whethah it's a burnt offerin' or a meal's vittles. He sho'ly will."

Lloyd crept away frightened. **It** seemed such an awful thing to see her mother cry.

All at once her bright, happy world had changed to such a strange, uncertain place. She felt as if all sorts of terrible things were about to happen.

She went into the parlour, and crawled into a dark corner under the piano, feeling that there was no place to go for comfort, since the one who had always kissed away her little troubles was so heart-broken herself.

There was a patter of soft feet across the carpet, and Fritz poked his sympathetic nose into her face. She put her arms around him, and laid her head against his curly back with a desolate sob.

It is pitiful to think how much imaginative children suffer through their wrong conception of things.

She had seen the little roll of bills in her mother's pocketbook. She had seen how much smaller it grew every time it was taken out to pay for the expensive wines and medicines that had to be bought so often. She had heard her mother tell the doctor that was all that stood between them and the poorhouse.

There was no word known to the Little Colonel that brought such thoughts of horror as the word poorhouse.

Her most vivid recollection of her life in New York was something that happened a few weeks before they left there. One day in the park she ran away from the maid, who, instead of Mom Beck, had taken charge of her that afternoon.

When the angry woman found her, she frightened her almost into a spasm by telling her what always happened to naughty children who ran away.

"They take all their pretty clothes off," she said, "and dress them up in old things made of bed-ticking. Then they take 'm to the poorhouse, where nobody but beggars live. They don't have anything to eat but cabbage and corn-dodger, and they have to eat that out of tin pans. And they just have a pile of straw to sleep in."

On their way home she had pointed out to the frightened child a poor woman who was grubbing in an ash-barrel.

"That's the way people get to look who live in poorhouses," she said.

It was this memory that was troubling the Little Colonel now.

"Oh, Fritz!" she whispered, with the tears running down her cheeks, "I can't beah to think of my pretty mothah goin' there. That woman's eyes were all red, an' her hair was jus' awful. She was so bony an' stahved-lookin'. It would jus' kill poah Papa Jack to lie on straw an' eat out of a tin pan. I know it would!"

When Mom Beck opened the door, hunting her, the room was so dark that she would have gone away if the dog had not come running out from under the piano.

"You heah, too, chile?" she asked, in surprise. "I have to go down now an' see if I can get Judy to come help to-morrow. Do you think you can undress yo'self to-night?"

"Of co'se," answered the Little Colonel. Mom Beck was in such a hurry to be off that she did not notice the tremble in the voice that answered her.

"Well, the can'le is lit in yo' room. So run along now like a nice little lady,

an' don't bothah yo' mamma. She got
her hands full already."

"All right," answered the child.

A quarter of an hour later she stood
in her little white nightgown with her
hand on the door-knob.

She opened the door just a crack and
peeped in. Her mother laid her finger
on her lips, and beckoned silently. In
another instant Lloyd was in her lap.
She had cried herself quiet in the dark
corner under the piano; but there was
something more pathetic in her eyes
than tears. It was the expression
of one who understood and sympa-
thized.

"Oh, mothah," she whispered, "we
does have such lots of troubles."

"Yes, chickabiddy, but I hope they
will soon be over now," was the answer, as the anxious face tried to smile
bravely for the child's sake. "Papa is

sleeping so nicely now he is sure to be better in the morning."

That comforted the Little Colonel some, but for days she was haunted by the fear of the poorhouse.

Every time her mother paid out any money she looked anxiously to see how much was still left. She wandered about the place, touching the trees and vines with caressing hands, feeling that she might soon have to leave them.

She loved them all so dearly, — every stick and stone, and even the stubby old snowball bushes that never bloomed.

Her dresses were outgrown and faded, but no one had any time or thought to spend on getting her new ones. A little hole began to come in the toe of each shoe.

She was still wearing her summer

sunbonnet, although the days were getting frosty.

She was a proud little thing. It mortified her for any one to see her looking so shabby. Still she uttered no word of complaint, for fear of lessening the little amount in the pocketbook that her mother had said stood between them and the poorhouse.

She sat with her feet tucked under her when any one called.

"I wouldn't mind bein' a little beggah so much myself," she thought, "but I jus' can't have my bu'ful sweet mothah lookin' like that awful red-eyed woman."

One day the doctor called Mrs. Sherman out into the hall. "I have just come from your father's," he said. "He is suffering from a severe attack of rheumatism. He is confined to his room, and is positively starving for company. He told me he would give anything in the world to have his little grandchild with him. There were tears in his eyes when he said it, and that means a good deal from him. He fairly idolizes her. The servants have told him she mopes around and is getting thin and pale. He is afraid she will come down with the fever, too. He told me to use any stratagem I liked to get her there. But I think it's better to tell you frankly how matters stand. It will do the child good to have a change, Elizabeth, and I solemnly think you ought to let her go, for a week at least."

"But, doctor, she has never been away from me a single night in her life. She'd die of homesickness, and I know she'll never consent to leave me. Then suppose Jack should get worse — "

"We'll suppose nothing of the kind," he interrupted, brusquely. "Tell Becky

to pack up her things. Leave Lloyd to
me. I'll get her consent without any
trouble."

"Come, Colonel," he called, as he left
the house. "I'm going to take you a
little ride."

No one ever knew what the kind old
fellow said to her to induce her to go
to her grandfather's.

She came back from her ride looking
brighter than she had in a long time.
She felt that in some way, although in
what way she could not understand, her
going would help them to escape the
dreaded poorhouse.

"Don't send Mom Beck with me,"
she pleaded, when the time came to
start. "You come with me, mothah."

Mrs. Sherman had not been past the
gate for weeks, but she could not refuse
the coaxing hands that clung to hers.

It was a dull, dreary day. There was

a chilling hint of snow in the damp air. The leaves whirled past them with a mournful rustling.

Mrs. Sherman turned up the collar of Lloyd's cloak.

"You must have a new one soon," she said, with a sigh. "Maybe one of mine could be made over for you. And those poor little shoes! I must think to send to town for a new pair."

The walk was over so soon. The Little Colonel's heart beat fast as they came in sight of the gate. She winked bravely to keep back the tears; for she had promised the doctor not to let her mother see her cry.

A week seemed such a long time to look forward to.

She clung to her mother's neck, feeling that she could never give her up so long.

"Tell me good-bye, baby dear," said

Mrs. Sherman, feeling that she could not trust herself to stay much longer. " It is too cold for you to stand here Run on, and I'll watch you till you get inside the door."

The Little Colonel started bravely down the avenue, with Fritz at her heels. Every few steps she turned to look back and kiss her hand.

Mrs. Sherman watched her through a blur of tears. It had been nearly seven years since she had last stood at that old gate. Such a crowd of memories came rushing up!

She looked again. There was a flutter of a white handkerchief as the Little Colonel and Fritz went up the steps. Then the great front door closed behind them.

CHAPTER VII.

THAT early twilight hour just before the lamps were lit was the lonesomest one the Little Colonel had ever spent. Her grandfather was asleep up-stairs. There was a cheery wood fire crackling on the hearth of the big fireplace in the hall, but the great house was so still. The corners were full of shadows.

She opened the front door with a wild longing to run away.

"Come, Fritz," she said, closing the door softly behind her, "let's go down to the gate."

The air was cold. She shivered as

they raced along under the bare branches of the locusts. She leaned against the gate, peering out through the bars. The road stretched white through the gathering darkness in the direction of the little cottage.

"Oh, I want to go home so bad!" she sobbed. "I want to see my mothah."

She laid her hand irresolutely on the latch, pushed the gate ajar, and then hesitated.

"No, I promised the doctah I'd stay," she thought. "He said I could help mothah and Papa Jack, both of 'em, by stayin' heah, an' I'll do it."

Fritz, who had pushed himself through the partly opened gate to rustle around among the dead leaves outside, came bounding back with something in his mouth.

"Heah, suh!" she called. "Give it to me!" He dropped a small gray kid glove in her outstretched hand. " Oh, it's mothah's!" she cried. " I reckon she dropped it when she was tellin' me good-bye. Oh, you deah old dog fo' findin' it."

She laid the glove against her cheek as fondly as if it had been her mother's soft hand. There was something wonderfully comforting in the touch.

As they walked slowly back toward the house she rolled it up and put it lovingly away in her tiny apron pocket.

All that week it was a talisman whose touch helped the homesick little soul to be brave and womanly.

When Maria, the coloured housekeeper, went into the hall to light the lamps, the Little Colonel was sitting on the big fur rug in front of the fire, talking contentedly to Fritz, who lay with his curly head in her lap.

" You all's goin' to have tea in the

Cun'l's room to - night," said Maria. "He tole me to tote it up soon as he rung the bell."

" There it goes now," cried the child, jumping up from the rug.

She followed Maria up the wide stairs. The Colonel was sitting in a large easy chair, wrapped in a gaily flowered dressing-gown, that made his hair look unusually white by contrast.

His dark eyes were intently watching the door. As it opened to let the Little Colonel pass through, a very tender smile lighted up his stern face.

"So you did come to see grandpa after all," he cried, triumphantly. "Come here and give me a kiss. Seems to me you've been staying away a mighty long time."

As she stood beside him with his arm around her, Walker came in with a tray full of dishes.

"We're going to have a regular little tea-party," said the Colonel.

Lloyd watched with sparkling eyes as Walker set out the rare old-fashioned dishes. There was a fat little silver sugar-bowl with a butterfly perched on each side to form the handles, and there was a slim, graceful cream-pitcher shaped like a lily.

"They belonged to your great-great-grandmother," said the Colonel, "and they're going to be yours some day if you grow up and have a house of your own."

The expression on her beaming face was worth a fortune to the Colonel.

When Walker pushed her chair up to the table, she turned to her grandfather with shining eyes.

"Oh, it's just like a pink story," she cried, clapping her hands. "The shades on the can'les, the icin' on the cake, an'

the posies in the bowl, — why, even the
jelly is that colah, too. Oh, my darlin'
little teacup! It's jus' like a pink rosebud. I'm so glad I came!"

The Colonel smiled at the success of
his plan. In the depths of his satisfaction he even had a plate of quail and
toast set down on the hearth for Fritz.

"This is the nicest pahty I evah was
at," remarked the Little Colonel, as
Walker helped her to jam the third
time.

Her grandfather chuckled.

"Blackberry jam always makes me
think of Tom," he said. "Did you ever
hear what your Uncle Tom did when he
was a little fellow in dresses?"

She shook her head gravely.

"Well, the children were all playing
hide-and-seek one day. They hunted
high and they hunted low after everybody else had been caught, but they

couldn't find Tom. At last they began to call, 'Home free! You can come home free!' but he did not come. When he had been hidden so long they were frightened about him, they went to their mother and told her he wasn't to be found anywhere. She looked down the well and behind the fire-boards in the fireplaces. They called and called till they were out of breath. Finally she thought of looking in the big dark pantry where she kept her fruit. There stood Mister Tom. He had opened a jar of blackberry jam, and was just going for it with both hands. The jam was all over his face and hair and little gingham apron, and even up his wrists. He was the funniest sight I ever saw."

The Little Colonel laughed heartily at his description, and begged for more stories. Before he knew it he was back

in the past with his little Tom and
Elizabeth.

Nothing could have entertained the
child more than these scenes he recalled
of her mother's childhood.

"All her old playthings are up in the
garret," he said, as they rose from the
table. "I'll have them brought down
to-morrow. There's a doll I brought
her from New Orleans once when she
was about your size. No telling what
it looks like now, but it was a beauty
when it was new."

Lloyd clapped her hands and spun
around the room like a top.

"Oh, I'm so glad I came!" she exclaimed for the third time. "What did
she call the doll, gran'fathah, do you re-
membah?"

"I never paid much attention to such
things," he answered, "but I do remember the name of this one, because

she named it for her mother, — Amanthis."

"Amanthis," repeated the child, dreamily, as she leaned against his knee. "I think that is a lovely name, gran'fathah. I wish they had called me that." She repeated it softly several times. "It sounds like the wind a-blowin' through white clovah, doesn't it?"

"It is a beautiful name to me, my child," answered the old man, laying his hand tenderly on her soft hair, "but not so beautiful as the woman who bore it. She was the fairest flower of all Kentucky. There never was another lived as sweet and gentle as your Grandmother Amanthis."

He stroked her hair absently, and gazed into the fire. He scarcely noticed when she slipped away from him.

She buried her face a moment in the

bowl of pink roses. Then she went to the window and drew back the curtain. Leaning her head against the window-sill, she began stringing on the thread of a tune the things that just then thrilled her with a sense of their beauty.

" Oh, the locus'-trees a-blowin'," she sang, softly. " An' the moon a-shinin' through them. An' the starlight an' pink roses; an' Amanthis — an' Amanthis! "

She hummed it over and over until Walker had finished carrying the dishes away.

It was a strange thing that the Colonel's unfrequent moods of tenderness were like those warm days that they call weather-breeders.

They were sure to be followed by a change of atmosphere. This time as the fierce rheumatic pain came back he stormed at Walker, and scolded him for everything he did and everything he left undone.

When Maria came up to put Lloyd to bed, Fritz was tearing around the room barking at his shadow.

"Put that dog out, M'ria!" roared the Colonel, almost crazy with its antics. "Take it down-stairs, and put it out of the house, I say! Nobody but a heathen would let a dog sleep in the house, any-way."

The homesick feeling began to creep over Lloyd again. She had expected to keep Fritz in her room at night for company. But for the touch of the little glove in her pocket, she would have said something ugly to her grandfather when he spoke so harshly.

His own ill humour was reflected in her scowl as she followed Maria down the stairs to drive Fritz out into the dark.

They stood a moment in the open door, after Maria had slapped him with her apron to make him go off the porch.

"Oh, look at the new moon!" cried Lloyd, pointing to the slender crescent in the autumn sky.

"I'se feared to, honey," answered Maria, "less I should see it through the trees. That 'ud bring me bad luck for a month, suah. I'll go out on the lawn where it's open, an' look at it ovah my right shouldah."

While they were walking backward down the path, intent on reaching a place where they could have an uninterrupted view of the moon, Fritz sneaked around to the other end of the porch.

No one was watching. He slipped into the house as noiselessly as his four soft feet could carry him.

Maria, going through the dark upper

hall, with a candle held high above her head and Lloyd clinging to her skirts, did not see a tasselled tail swinging along in front of her. It disappeared under the big bed when she led Lloyd into the room next the old Colonel's.

The child felt very sober while she was being put to bed.

The furniture was heavy and dark. An ugly portrait of a cross old man in a wig frowned at her from over the mantel. The dancing firelight made his eyes frightfully lifelike.

The bed was so high she had to climb on a chair to get in. She heard Maria's heavy feet go shuffling down the stairs. A door banged. Then it was so still she could hear the clock tick in the next room.

It was the first time in all her life that her mother had not come to kiss her good night.

Her lips quivered, and a big tear rolled down on the pillow.

She reached out to the chair beside her bed, where her clothes were hanging, and felt in her apron pocket for the little glove. She sat up in bed, and looked at it in the dim firelight. Then she held it against her face. "Oh, I want my mothah! I want my mothah!" she sobbed, in a heart-broken whisper.

Laying her head on her knees, she began to cry quietly, but with great sobs that nearly choked her.

There was a rustling under the bed. She lifted her wet face in alarm. Then she smiled through her tears, for there was Fritz, her own dear dog, and not an unknown horror waiting to grab her.

He stood on his hind legs, eagerly trying to lap away her tears with his friendly red tongue.

She clasped him in her arms with an

ecstatic hug. "Oh, you're such a comfort!" she whispered. "I can go to sleep now."

She spread her apron on the bed, and motioned him to jump. With one spring he was beside her.

It was nearly midnight when the door from the Colonel's room was noiselessly opened.

The old man stirred the fire gently until it burst into a bright flame. Then he turned to the bed. "You rascal!" he whispered, looking at Fritz, who raised his head quickly with a threatening look in his wicked eyes.

Lloyd lay with one hand stretched out, holding the dog's protecting paw. The other held something against her tear-stained cheek.

"What under the sun!" he thought, as he drew it gently from her fingers. The little glove lay across his hand, slim and aristocratic-looking. He knew instinctively whose it was. " Poor little thing's been crying," he thought. " She wants Elizabeth. And so do I! And so do I!" his heart cried out with bitter longing. " It's never been like home since she left."

He laid the glove back on her pillow, and went to his room.

" If Jack Sherman should die," he said to himself many times that night, " then she would come home again. Oh, little daughter, little daughter! why did you ever leave me? "

CHAPTER VIII.

THE first thing that greeted the Little Colonel's eyes when she opened them next morning was her mother's old doll. Maria had laid it on the pillow beside her.

It was beautifully dressed, although in a queer, old-fashioned style that seemed very strange to the child.

She took it up with careful fingers, remembering its great age. Maria had warned her not to waken her grandfather, so she admired it in whispers.

"Jus' think, Fritz," she exclaimed, "this doll has seen my Gran'mothah Amanthis, an' it's named for her. My mothah wasn't any bigger'n me when she played with it. I think it is the loveliest doll I evah saw in my whole life."

Fritz gave a jealous bark.

" Sh! " commanded his little mistress. " Didn't you heah M'ria say, ' Fo' de Lawd's sake don't wake up ole Marse? ' Why don't you mind? "

The Colonel was not in the best of humours after such a wakeful night, but the sight of her happiness made him smile in spite of himself, when she danced into his room with the doll.

She had eaten an early breakfast and gone back up - stairs to examine the other toys that were spread out in her room.

The door between the two rooms was ajar. All the time he was dressing and taking his coffee he could hear her talking to some one. He supposed it was Maria. But as he glanced over his mail he heard the Little Colonel saying, "May Lilly, do you know about Billy Goat Gruff? Do you want me to tell you that story?"

He leaned forward until he could look through the narrow opening of the door. Two heads were all he could see, — Lloyd's, soft-haired and golden, May Lilly's, covered with dozens of tightly braided little black tails.

He was about to order May Lilly back to the cabin, when he remembered the scene that followed the last time he had done so. He concluded to keep quiet and listen.

"Billy Goat Gruff was so fat," the story went on, "jus' as fat as gran'-fathah."

The Colonel glanced up with an amused smile at the fine figure reflected in an opposite mirror.

"Trip-trap, trip-trap, went Billy Goat

Gruff's little feet ovah the bridge to the giant's house."

Just at this point Walker, who was putting things in order, closed the door between the rooms.

" Open that door, you black rascal! " called the Colonel, furious at the interruption.

In his haste to obey, Walker knocked over a pitcher of water that had been left on the floor beside the wash-stand.

Then the Colonel yelled at him to be quick about mopping it up, so that by the time the door was finally opened, Lloyd was finishing her story.

The Colonel looked in just in time to see her put her hands to her temples, with her forefingers protruding from her forehead like horns. She said in a deep voice, as she brandished them at May Lilly, " With my two long speahs I'll poke yo' eyeballs through yo' yeahs."

The little darky fell back giggling. "That sut'n'y was like a billy-goat. We had one once that 'ud make a body step around mighty peart. It slip up behine me one mawnin' on the poach, an' fo' awhile I thought my haid was buss open suah. I got up toreckly, though, an' I cotch him, and when I done got through, Mistah Billy-goat feel po'ly moah'n a week. He sut'n'y did."

Walker grinned, for he had witnessed the scene.

Just then Maria put her head in at the door to say, "May Lilly, yo' mammy's callin' you."

Lloyd and Fritz followed her noisily down-stairs. Then for nearly an hour it was very quiet in the great house.

The Colonel, looking out of the window, could see Lloyd playing hide-and-seek with Fritz under the bare locust-trees.

When she came in her cheeks were glowing from her run in the frosty air. Her eyes shone like stars, and her face was radiant.

" See what I've found down in the dead leaves," she cried. " A little blue violet, bloomin' all by itself."

She brought a tiny cup from the next room, that belonged to the set of doll dishes, and put the violet in it.

" There! " she said, setting it on the table at her grandfather's elbow. " Now I'll put Amanthis in this chair, where you can look at her, an' you won't get lonesome while I'm playing outdoors."

He drew her toward him and kissed her.

" Why, how cold your hands are! " he exclaimed. " Staying in this warm room all the time makes me forget it is so wintry outdoors. I don't believe you are dressed warmly enough. You ought not to wear sunbonnets this time of year."

Then for the first time he noticed her outgrown cloak and shabby shoes.

"What are you wearing these old clothes for?" he said, impatiently. "Why didn't they dress you up when you were going visiting? It isn't showing proper respect to send you off in the oldest things you've got."

It was a sore point with the Little Colonel. It hurt her pride enough to have to wear old clothes without being scolded for it. Besides, she felt that in some way her mother was being blamed for what could not be helped.

"They's the best I've got," she answered, proudly choking back the tears. "I don't need any new ones, 'cause maybe we'll be goin' away pretty soon."

"Going away!" he echoed, blankly. "Where?"

She did not answer until he repeated the question. Then she turned her back on him, and started toward the door. The tears she was too proud to let him see were running down her face.

"We's goin' to the poah-house," she exclaimed, defiantly, "jus' as soon as the money in the pocketbook is used up. It was nearly gone when I came away."

Here she began to sob, as she fumbled at the door she could not see to open.

"I'm goin' home to my mothah right now. She loves me if my clothes are old and ugly."

"Why, Lloyd," called the Colonel, amazed and distressed by her sudden burst of grief. "Come here to grandpa. Why didn't you tell me so before?"

The face, the tone, the outstretched arm, all drew her irresistibly to him. It was a relief to lay her head on his shoulder, and unburden herself of the fear that had haunted her so many days.

With her arms around his neck, and the precious little head held close to his heart, the old Colonel was in such a softened mood that he would have promised anything to comfort her.

"There, there," he said, soothingly, stroking her hair with a gentle hand, when she had told him all her troubles. "Don't you worry about that, my dear. Nobody is going to eat out of tin pans and sleep on straw. Grandpa just won't let them."

She sat up and wiped her eyes on her apron. "But Papa Jack would die befo' he'd take help from you," she wailed. "An' so would mothah. I heard her tell the doctah so."

The tender expression on the Colonel's face changed to one like flint, but he kept on stroking her hair.

"People sometimes change their minds," he said, grimly. "I wouldn't worry over a little thing like that if I were you. Don't you want to run downstairs and tell M'ria to give you a piece of cake?"

"Oh, yes," she exclaimed, smiling up at him. "I'll bring you some, too."

When the first train went into Louisville that afternoon, Walker was on board with an order in his pocket to one of the largest dry goods establishments in the city. When he came out again, that evening, he carried a large box into the Colonel's room.

Lloyd's eyes shone as she looked into it. There was an elegant fur-trimmed cloak, a pair of dainty shoes, and a muff that she caught up with a shriek of delight.

"What kind of a thing is this?" grumbled the Colonel, as he took out a hat that had been carefully packed in one corner of the box. "I told them to send the most stylish thing they had. It looks like a scarecrow," he continued, as he set it askew on the child's head.

She snatched it off to look at it herself. "Oh, it's jus' like Emma Louise Wyfo'd's!" she exclaimed. "You didn't put it on straight. See! This is the way it goes."

She climbed up in front of the mirror, and put it on as she had seen Emma Louise wear hers.

"Well, it's a regular Napoleon hat," exclaimed the Colonel, much pleased. "So little girls nowadays have taken to wearing soldier's caps, have they? It's right becoming to you with your short hair. Grandpa is real proud of his 'little Colonel.'"

She gave him the military salute he had taught her, and then ran to throw

her arms around him. "Oh, gran'-fathah!" she exclaimed, between her kisses, "you'se jus' as good as Santa Claus, every bit."

The Colonel's rheumatism was better next day; so much better that toward evening he walked down-stairs into the long drawing-room. The room had not been illuminated in years as it was that night.

Every wax taper was lighted in the silver candelabra, and the dim old mirrors multiplied their lights on every side. A great wood fire threw a cheerful glow over the portraits and the frescoed ceiling. All the linen covers had been taken from the furniture.

Lloyd, who had never seen this room except with the chairs shrouded and the blinds down, came running in presently. She was bewildered at first by the change. Then she began walking softly

around the room, examining everything.

In one corner stood a tall, gilded harp
that her grandmother had played in her
girlhood. The heavy cover had kept it
fair and untarnished through all the
years it had stood unused. To the
child's beauty-loving eyes it seemed the
loveliest thing she had ever seen.

She stood with her hands clasped
behind her as her gaze wandered from
its pedals to the graceful curves of its
tall frame. It shone like burnished
gold in the soft firelight.

"Oh, gran'fathah!" she asked at last
in a low, reverent tone, "where did you
get it? Did an angel leave it heah fo'
you?"

He did not answer for a moment.
Then he said, huskily, as he looked up
at a portrait over the mantel, "Yes, my
darling, an angel did leave it here. She

always was one. Come here to grandpa."

He took her on his knee, and pointed up to the portrait. The same harp was in the picture. Standing beside it, with one hand resting on its shining strings, was a young girl all in white.

"That's the way she looked the first time I ever saw her," said the Colonel, dreamily. "A June rose in her hair, and another at her throat; and her soul looked right out through those great, dark eyes — the purest, sweetest soul God ever made! My beautiful Amanthis!"

"My bu'ful Amanthis!" repeated the child, in an awed whisper.

She sat gazing into the lovely young face for a long time, while the old man seemed lost in dreams.

"Gran'fathah," she said at length, patting his cheek to attract his attention, and then nodding toward the portrait, " did she love my mothah like my mothah loves me? "

" Certainly, my dear," was the gentle reply.

It was the twilight hour, when the homesick feeling always came back strongest to Lloyd.

" Then I jus' know that if my bu'ful gran'mothah Amanthis could come down out of that frame, she'd go straight and put her arms around my mothah an' kiss away all her sorry feelin's."

The Colonel fidgeted uncomfortably in his chair a moment. Then to his great relief the tea-bell rang.

CHAPTER IX.

VERY evening after that during Lloyd's visit the fire burned on the hearth of the long drawing-room. All the wax candles were lighted, and the vases were kept full of flowers, fresh from the conservatory.

She loved to steal into the room before her grandfather came down, and carry on imaginary conversations with the old portraits.

Tom's handsome, boyish face had the greatest attraction for her. His eyes looked down so smilingly into hers that she felt he surely understood every word she said to him.

Once Walker overheard her saying, "Uncle Tom, I'm goin' to tell you a story 'bout Billy Goat Gruff."

Peeping into the room, he saw the child looking earnestly up at the picture, with her hands clasped behind her, as she began to repeat her favourite story. "It do beat all," he said to himself, "how one little chile like that can wake up a whole house. She's the life of the place."

The last evening of her visit, as the Colonel was coming down-stairs he heard the faint vibration of a harp-string. It was the first time Lloyd had ever ventured to touch one. He paused on the steps opposite the door, and looked in.

"Heah, Fritz," she was saying, "you get up on the sofa, an' be the company, an' I'll sing fo' you."

Fritz, on the rug before the fire,

opened one sleepy eye and closed it
again. She stamped her foot and repeated her order. He paid no attention.
Then she picked him up bodily, and,
with much puffing and pulling, lifted
him into a chair.

He waited until she had gone back
to the harp, and then, with one spring,
disappeared under the sofa.

" N'm min'," she said, in a disgusted
tone. " I'll pay you back, mistah."
Then she looked up at the portrait.
" Uncle Tom," she said, " you be the
company, an' I'll play fo' you."

Her fingers touched the strings so
lightly that there was no discord in the
random tones. Her voice carried the
air clear and true, and the faint trembling of the harp-strings interfered with
the harmony no more than if a wandering breeze had been tangled in them as
it passed.

"Sing me the songs that to me were so deah
  Long, long ago, long ago.
 Tell me the tales I delighted to heah
  Long, long ago, long ago."

The sweet little voice sang it to the end without missing a word. It was the lullaby her mother oftenest sang to her.

The Colonel, who had sat down on the steps to listen, wiped his eyes.

"My 'long ago' is all that I have left to me," he thought, bitterly, "for to-morrow this little one, who brings back my past with every word and gesture, will leave me, too. Why can't that Jack Sherman die while he's about it, and let me have my own back again?"

That question recurred to him many times during the week after Lloyd's departure. He missed her happy voice at every turn. He missed her bright face at the table. The house seemed so big and desolate without her. He ordered all the covers put back on the drawing-room furniture, and the door locked as before.

It was a happy moment for the Little Colonel when she was lifted down from Maggie Boy at the cottage gate.

She went dancing into the house, so glad to find herself in her mother's arms that she forgot all about the new cloak and muff that had made her so proud and happy.

She found her father propped up among the pillows, his fever all gone, and the old mischievous twinkle in his eyes.

He admired her new clothes extravagantly, paying her joking compliments until her face beamed; but when she had danced off to find Mom Beck, he turned to his wife. "Elizabeth," he said, wonderingly, "what do you suppose the old fellow gave her clothes for? I don't like it. I'm no beggar if I have lost lots of money. After all that's passed between us I don't feel like taking anything from his hands, or letting my child do it, either."

To his great surprise she laid her head down on his pillow beside his and burst into tears.

"Oh, Jack," she sobbed, "I spent the last dollar this morning. I wasn't going to tell you, but I don't know what is to become of us. He gave Lloyd those things because she was just in rags, and I couldn't afford to get anything new."

He looked perplexed. "Why, I brought home so much," he said, in a distressed tone. "I knew I was in for a long siege of sickness, but I was sure there was enough to tide us over that."

She raised her head. "You brought money home!" she replied, in surprise. "I hoped you had, and looked through

all your things, but there was only a
little change in one of your pockets.
You must have imagined it when you
were delirious."

"What!" he cried, sitting bolt up-
right, and then sinking weakly back
among the pillows. "You poor child!
You don't mean to tell me you have
been skimping along all these weeks on
just that check I sent you before start-
ing home?"

"Yes," she sobbed, her face still
buried in the pillow. She had borne the
strain of continued anxiety so long that
she could not stop her tears, now they
had once started.

It was with a very thankful heart she
watched him take a pack of letters from
the coat she brought to his bedside, and
draw out a sealed envelope.

"Well, I never once thought of looking among those letters for money," she

exclaimed, as he held it up with a smile.

His investments of the summer before had prospered beyond his greatest hopes, he told her. "Brother Rob is looking after my interests out West, as well as his own," he explained, " and as his father-in-law is the grand mogul of the place, I have the inside track. Then that firm I went security for in New York is nearly on its feet again, and I'll have back every dollar I ever paid out for them. Nobody ever lost anything by those men in the long run. We'll be on top again by this time next year, little wife; so don't borrow any more trouble on that score."

The doctor made his last visit that afternoon. It really seemed as if there would never be any more dark days at the little cottage.

" The clouds have all blown away and

left us their silver linings," said Mrs. Sherman the day her husband was able to go out-of-doors for the first time. He walked down to the post-office, and brought back a letter from the West. It had such encouraging reports of his business that he was impatient to get back to it. He wrote a reply early in the afternoon, and insisted on going to mail it himself.

"I'll never get my strength back," he protested, "unless I have more exercise."

It was a cold, gray November day. A few flakes of snow were falling when he started.

"I'll stop and rest at the Tylers'," he called back, "so don't be uneasy if I'm out some time."

After he left the post-office the fresh air tempted him to go farther than he had intended. At a long distance from his home his strength seemed suddenly to desert him. The snow began to fall in earnest. Numb with cold, he groped his way back to the house, almost fainting from exhaustion.

Lloyd was blowing soap-bubbles when she saw him come in and fall heavily across the couch. The ghastly pallor of his face and his closed eyes frightened her so that she dropped the little clay pipe she was using. As she stooped to pick up the broken pieces, her mother's cry startled her still more. "Lloyd, run call Becky, quick, quick! Oh, he's dying!"

Lloyd gave one more terrified look and ran to the kitchen, screaming for Mom Beck. No one was there.

The next instant she was running bareheaded as fast as she could go up the road to Locust. She was confident of finding help there.

The snowflakes clung to her hair and blew against her soft cheeks. All she could see was her mother wringing her hands, and her father's white face. When she burst into the house where the Colonel sat reading by the fire, she was so breathless at first that she could only gasp when she tried to speak.

"Come quick!" she cried. "Papa Jack's a-dyin'! Come stop him!"

At her first impetuous words the Colonel was on his feet. She caught him by the hand and led him to the door before he fully realized what she wanted. Then he drew back. She was impatient at the slightest delay, and only half answered his questions.

"Oh, come, gran'fathah!" she pleaded. "Don't wait to talk!" But he held her until he had learned all the circumstances. He was convinced by what she told him that both Lloyd and her mother were unduly alarmed. When he found that no one had sent for him, but that the child had come of her own accord, he refused to go.

He did not believe that the man was dying, and he did not intend to step aside one inch from the position he had taken. For seven years he had kept the vow he made when he swore to be a stranger to his daughter. He would keep it for seventy times seven years if need be.

She looked at him perfectly bewildered. She had been so accustomed to his humouring her slightest whims, that it had never occurred to her he would fail to help in a time of such distress.

"Why, gran'fathah," she began, her lips trembling piteously. Then her whole expression changed. Her face grew startlingly white, and her eyes seemed so big and black. The Colonel looked at her in surprise. He had never seen a child in such a passion before. "I hate you! I hate you!" she exclaimed, all in a tremble. "You's a cruel, wicked man. I'll nevah come heah again, nevah! nevah! nevah!"

The tears rolled down her cheeks as she banged the door behind her and ran down the avenue, her little heart so full of grief and disappointment that she felt she could not possibly bear it.

For more than an hour the Colonel walked up and down the room, unable to shut out the anger and disappointment of that little face.

He knew she was too much like himself ever to retract her words. She would never come back. He never knew until that hour how much he loved her, or how much she had come to mean in his life. She was gone hopelessly beyond recall, unless —

He unlocked the door of the drawing-room and went in. A faint breath of dried rose-leaves greeted him. He walked over to the empty fireplace and looked up at the sweet face of the portrait a long time. Then he leaned his arm on the mantel and bowed his head on it. "Oh, Amanthis," he groaned, "tell me what to do."

Lloyd's own words came back to him. "She'd go right straight an' put her arms around my mothah an' kiss away all the sorry feelin's."

It was a long time he stood there. The battle between his love and pride was a hard one. At last he raised his head and saw that the short winter day was almost over. Without waiting to order his horse he started off in the falling snow toward the cottage.

CHAPTER X.

GOOD many forebodings crowded into the Colonel's mind as he walked hurriedly on. He wondered how he would be received. What if Jack Sherman had died after all? What if Elizabeth should refuse to see him? A dozen times before he reached the gate he pictured to himself the probable scene of their meeting.

He was out of breath and decidedly disturbed in mind when he walked up the path. As he paused on the porch steps, Lloyd came running around the house carrying her parrot on a broom.

Her hair was blowing around her rosy

face under the Napoleon hat she wore, and she was singing.

The last two hours had made a vast change in her feelings. Her father had only fainted from exhaustion.

When she came running back from Locust, she was afraid to go in the house, lest what she dreaded most had happened while she was gone. She opened the door timidly and peeped in. Her father's eyes were open. Then she heard him speak. She ran into the room, and, burying her head in her mother's lap, sobbed out the story of her visit to Locust.

To her great surprise her father began to laugh, and laughed so heartily as she repeated her saucy speech to her grandfather, that it took the worst sting out of her disappointment.

All the time the Colonel had been fighting his pride among the memories of the dim old drawing-room, Lloyd had been playing with Fritz and Polly.

Now as she came suddenly face to face with her grandfather, she dropped the disgusted bird in the snow, and stood staring at him with startled eyes. If he had fallen out of the sky she could not have been more astonished.

"Where is your mother, child?" he asked, trying to speak calmly. With a backward look, as if she could not believe the evidence of her own sight, she led the way into the hall.

"Mothah! Mothah!" she called, pushing open the parlour door. "Come heah, quick!"

The Colonel, taking the hat from his white head, and dropping it on the floor, took an expectant step forward. There was a slight rustle, and Elizabeth stood in the doorway. For just a moment they looked into each other's faces. Then the Colonel held out his arm.

"Little daughter," he said, in a tremulous voice. The love of a lifetime seemed to tremble in those two words.

In an instant her arms were around his neck, and he was "kissing away the sorry feelin's" as tenderly as the lost Amanthis could have done.

As soon as Lloyd began to realize what was happening, her face grew radiant. She danced around in such excitement that Fritz barked wildly.

"Come an' see Papa Jack, too," she cried, leading him into the next room.

Whatever deep - rooted prejudices Jack Sherman may have had, they were unselfishly put aside after one look into his wife's happy face.

He raised himself on his elbow as the

dignified old soldier crossed the room. The white hair, the empty sleeve, the remembrance of all the old man had lost, and the thought that after all he was Elizabeth's father, sent a very tender feeling through the younger man's heart.

"Will you take my hand, sir?" he asked, sitting up and offering it in his straightforward way.

"Of co'se he will!" exclaimed Lloyd, who still clung to her grandfather's arm. "Of co'se he will!"

"I have been too near death to harbour ill will any longer," said the younger man, as their hands met in a strong, forgiving clasp.

The old Colonel smiled grimly.

"I had thought that even death itself could not make me give in," he said, "but I've had to make a complete surrender to the Little Colonel."

That Christmas there was such a celebration at Locust that May Lilly and Henry Clay nearly went wild in the general excitement of the preparation. Walker hung up cedar and holly and mistletoe till the big house looked like a bower. Maria bustled about, airing rooms and bringing out stores of linen and silver.

The Colonel himself filled the great punch-bowl that his grandfather had brought from Virginia.

" I'm glad we're goin' to stay heah to-night," said Lloyd, as she hung up her stocking Christmas Eve. " It will be so much easiah fo' Santa Claus to get down these big chimneys."

In the morning when she found four tiny stockings hanging beside her own, overflowing with candy for Fritz, her happiness was complete.

That night there was a tree in the

drawing-room that reached to the frescoed ceiling. When May Lilly came in to admire it and get her share from its loaded branches, Lloyd came skipping up to her. "Oh, I'm goin' to live heah all wintah," she cried. "Mom Beck's goin' to stay heah with me, too, while mothah an' Papa Jack go down South where the alligatahs live. Then when they get well an' come back, Papa Jack is goin' to build a house on the othah side of the lawn. I'm to live in both places at once; mothah said so."

There were music and light, laughing voices and happy hearts in the old home that night. It seemed as if the old place had awakened from a long dream and found itself young again.

The plan the Little Colonel unfolded to May Lilly was carried out in every detail. It seemed a long winter to the child, but it was a happy one. There were not so many displays of temper now that she was growing older, but the letters that went southward every week were full of her odd speeches and mischievous pranks. The old Colonel found it hard to refuse her anything. If it had not been for Mom Beck's decided ways, the child would have been sadly spoiled.

At last the spring came again. The pewees sang in the cedars. The dandelions sprinkled the roadsides like stars. The locust-trees tossed up the white spray of their fragrant blossoms with every wave of their green boughs.

" They'll soon be heah! They'll soon be heah!" chanted the Little Colonel every day.

The morning they came she had been down the avenue a dozen times to look for them before the carriage had **even** started to meet them.

"Walkah," she called, "cut me a big locus' bough. I want to wave it fo' a flag!"

Just as he dropped a branch down at her feet, she caught the sound of wheels. "Hurry, gran'fathah," she called; "they's comin'." But the old Colonel had already started on toward the gate to meet them. The carriage stopped, and in a moment more Papa Jack was tossing Lloyd up in his arms, while the old Colonel was helping Elizabeth to alight.

"Isn't this a happy mawnin'?" exclaimed the Little Colonel, as she leaned from her seat on her father's shoulder to kiss his sunburned cheek.

"A very happy morning," echoed her grandfather, as he walked on toward the house with Elizabeth's hand clasped close in his own.

Long after they had passed up the

steps the old locusts kept echoing the Little Colonel's words. Years ago they had showered their fragrant blossoms in this same path to make a sweet white way for Amanthis's little feet to tread when the Colonel brought home his bride.

They had dropped their tribute on the coffin-lid when Tom was carried home under their drooping branches. The soldier-boy had loved them so, that a little cluster had been laid on the breast of the gray coat he wore.

Night and day they had guarded this old home like silent sentinels that loved it well.

Now, as they looked down on the united family, a thrill passed through them to their remotest bloom - tipped branches.

It sounded only like a faint rustling of leaves, but it was the locusts whispering together. " The children have come home at last," they kept repeating. " What a happy morning! Oh, what a happy morning! "